Investigating Invertebrates

Heather Hammonds

Chapter 1

Learning About Invertebrates

Today we learned about invertebrates. Mom said there were lots of invertebrates in our garden, so we went outside to find some.

We looked at them with our magnifying glass. We went on the Internet and learned more about invertebrates, too!

What Are Invertebrates?

Invertebrates are animals that have no backbones. Insects and spiders are invertebrates. They have hard skin on the outside of their bodies. This hard skin is called an **exoskeleton.**

a fly

a spider

Worms and snails are invertebrates with soft bodies. Sometimes they have a shell to protect their bodies.

Lots of invertebrates live in the sea.

a sea slug

3

Chapter 2

Our First Invertebrate

We saw our first invertebrate above our front door. It was a daddy longlegs spider.

Daddy longlegs spiders hang upside down from their webs. Then they catch insects and other spiders to eat.

Daddy longlegs bite their **prey**, but their fangs are too small to bite people.

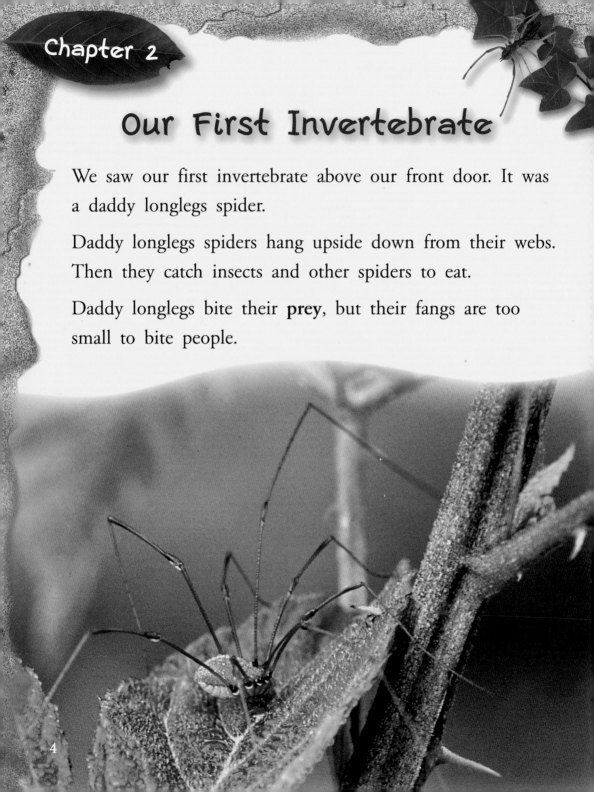

Spiders

Spiders have:

- two body parts
- eight legs
- fangs
- feelers
- **spinnerets,** for spinning webs

The bird-eating spider is the largest spider in the world.
It eats small animals such as frogs and insects.

Some big spiders are kept as pets!

5

Chapter 3

Helpful Beetles

I found an invertebrate that helps us in the garden. It was a ladybug, a kind of beetle. Ladybugs eat lots of small insects that eat our plants. They eat lots of insect eggs, too. Most insects do not eat ladybugs because they have an unpleasant taste.

Beetles

Beetles are insects. All insects are invertebrates.

Insects have:

- three body parts
- two antennae
- six legs
- an exoskeleton

a jewel beetle

Beetles have wings, too. Some beetles are very small, while other beetles are huge!

There are more kinds of beetles than any other insect.

Chapter 4

Pretty Butterflies

Next we saw an invertebrate in our vegetable garden. Mom said it was a cabbage white butterfly. Cabbage white butterflies look pretty, but they are a pest. They lay eggs on the leaves of some vegetables. Caterpillars hatch from the eggs and eat the vegetables.

The Butterfly Life Cycle

1. Female butterfly lays eggs.

2. Caterpillars hatch from the eggs.

3. The caterpillars grow.

4. Each caterpillar becomes a **pupa**, inside a hard case.

5. Each pupa turns into a butterfly.

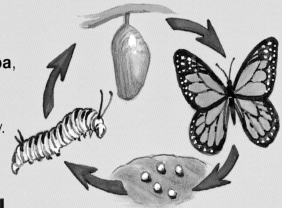

Moths have the same life cycle as butterflies.

a hawkmoth

Chapter 5

Noisy Neighbors

We heard a loud buzzing sound in a tree. Invertebrates were in the tree making the sound. They were cicadas.

Mom says male cicadas make a buzzing sound when they are calling to female cicadas.

They make the sound with drum-like parts of their bodies, called **tymbals.**

The Cicada Life Cycle

1. Female cicadas lay eggs on trees.

2. Young cicadas hatch from the eggs.

3. They drop from the trees and burrow underground. Cicadas
   live underground for several years.

4. Then they come out of the ground and **shed** their skin.
   They have grown wings and become adult cicadas!

Cicada skins are
sometimes found
on trees.

Chapter 6

A Nest of Ants

We saw some invertebrates walking in a line on the garden path. They were ants. We followed the line of ants and found their nest. There were lots of ants going in and out of the nest. Some of the ants were carrying bits of food to the nest.

Ants

Ants live in big **colonies.** Each ant colony has a queen ant that lays lots of eggs. Worker ants look after the queen and the eggs. They also do other jobs, such as finding food and building the nest. Male ants **mate** with the queen.

Bull ants are some of the biggest ants in the world.

Chapter 7

Under a Log

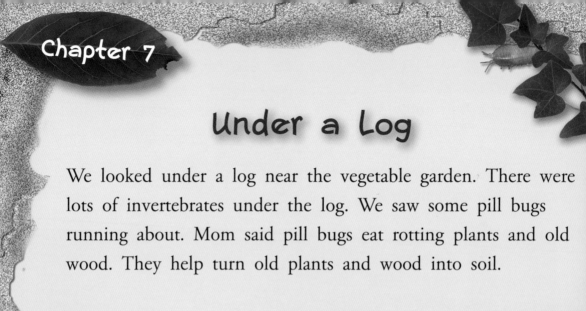

We looked under a log near the vegetable garden. There were lots of invertebrates under the log. We saw some pill bugs running about. Mom said pill bugs eat rotting plants and old wood. They help turn old plants and wood into soil.

Pill bugs

Pill bugs are found in damp places all over the world. A pill bug is also called a sow bug, a roly-poly bug, or a wood louse.

Pill bugs have:

- a flat body
- two antennae
- seven pairs of legs
- a hard shell made up of several parts

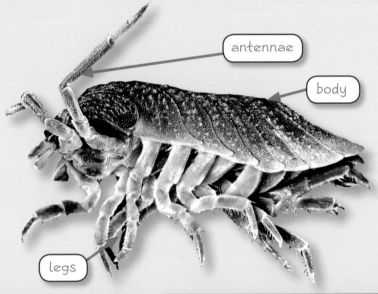

antennae

body

legs

Pill bugs can roll themselves into a ball for protection.

15

Chapter 8

Lots of Legs

There were some invertebrates with lots of legs under the log. I saw some centipedes and some millipedes. Mom said that centipedes eat pill bugs and other small animals. Most millipedes eat rotting plants.

a centipede

a millipede

Centipedes and Millipedes

Centipedes and millipedes have long, thin bodies. Centipedes have one pair of legs on each body part. Millipedes have two pairs of legs on each body part. Centipedes have poisonous claws behind their head. They bite the small animals they catch and eat.

a millipede

The largest centipede in the world grows to over 11 inches long!

17

Chapter 9

Slippery Slugs and Snails

Next we saw some invertebrates hiding under a rock. They were slugs and snails. Mom said slugs and snails have a big foot under their bodies. They make slime. The slime helps them to move along on their big foot. The slugs and snails leave a shiny trail behind them as they move along.

a snail

18

Slugs and Snails

Slugs and snails have soft, moist bodies. They have two pairs of **tentacles** on their heads with eyes on top of the longest tentacles. Slugs and snails hide in damp places when the weather is warm. When it is cool, they come out to look for food.

a slug

Some slugs and snails live in the sea.

Chapter 10

Earthworms in the Soil

I got a shovel and dug up some soil in a flower bed. There were earthworms in the soil. Earthworms are invertebrates. Mom said earthworms make lots of tunnels that let water and air into soil. This helps plants to grow.

Castings from earthworms are good for the soil, too.

Earthworms

Earthworms have:

- long, thin bodies
- tiny hairs on their bodies to help them move through the soil
- no eyes or ears
- mouths at one end of their bodies
- openings at the other end of their bodies

The giant Gippsland earthworm in Australia grows to more than six feet long!

Chapter 11

Interesting Invertebrates

We found other interesting invertebrates on the Internet.

Sea Invertebrates

Giant Squid

Giant squid are the biggest invertebrates in the world. They live deep under the sea. Sometimes giant squid are caught in fishing nets.

Brittle Star

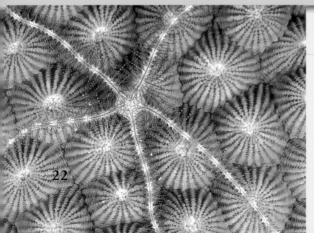

Brittle stars live at the outer edges of rocky **reefs**. They have five thin arms. If a brittle star's arm breaks off, it grows another one!

22

Interesting Insects

Honeybee

Honeybees live together in a hive. Honeybees collect nectar to make honey. They make more than enough honey to feed all the bees in their hive.

Mosquito

Female mosquitoes suck blood from people or animals before they lay their eggs. Male mosquitoes do not suck blood. Instead they drink nectar from plants.

There are more invertebrates than any other kind of animal in the world!

23

Glossary

castings worm droppings

colonies groups that live together

exoskeleton the hard outer covering on some invertebrates

mate when a male and female animal join together to make babies

prey an animal that is caught and eaten by another animal

pupa the part of a butterfly or other insect's life cycle when it is not active, and is changing its body shape

reefs narrow ridges of rocks, sand, or coral at or near the top of the water

shed to take something off or leave it behind, such as insect skin

spinnerets the parts of a spider's body with which it spins its web

tentacles long growths on the head of an animal

tymbals drum-like parts of the sides of a cicada's body that make a buzzing sound

Index